IT IS HALLOWEEN!

WRITTEN BY LAURA APPLETON-SMITH
ILLUSTRATED BY PRESTON NEEL

Laura Appleton-Smith was born and raised in Vermont and has fun memories of Halloween
in her home town–trick-or-treating with her father and friends in costumes that her mother helped her make.
Laura is a primary teacher with a degree in English from Middlebury College.
She lives in New Hampshire with her husband Terry.

Preston Neel was born in Macon, GA. Greatly inspired by Dr. Seuss, he decided to become an artist at the age of four.
Preston's advanced art studies took place at the Academy of Art College San Francisco.
Now Preston pursues his career in art with the hope of being an inspiration himself;
particularly to children who want to explore their endless bounds.

A Book to Remember™
Published by Flyleaf Publishing
Post Office Box 287, Lyme, NH 03768

For orders or information, contact us at **(800) 449-7006**.
Please visit our website at **www.flyleafpublishing.com**

Second printing, revised
Library of Congress Catalog Card Number: 99-90704
Hard cover ISBN-13: 978-1-929262-19-9
Hard cover ISBN-10: 1-929262-19-1
Soft cover ISBN-13: 978-0-9658246-4-4
Soft cover ISBN-10: 0-9658246-4-0

For Dad and Barbara, who still love to dress up.

LAS

To Daddy.

PN

JACK-O-LANTERNS

It is Halloween and Jon and Ellen and Gramps
pick pumpkins.

They pick and pick until they fill Gramps' red wagon.

Gramps helps Ellen and Jon cut the biggest pumpkins into jack-o-lanterns.

The jack-o-lanterns will sit on the front steps for Halloween night.

THE ATTIC

Nana asks Jon and Ellen to visit the attic with her.

"Do not run," Nana tells them as they skip up
the attic steps.

Nana's cat Tom runs up the steps in front of them.

Nana clicks on the attic lamp.

In the back of the attic is a big black trunk with a brass lock on it.

DRESS-UPS

"This is the Halloween trunk," Nana tells Ellen
and Jon as she unlocks the lock and lifts the lid.

The Halloween trunk is filled with hats and masks
to dress-up in.

Jon picks a ten-gallon hat, a bandana, and a black mask.

Ellen picks a mask and a red bonnet.

Nana hands a vest to Jon.

She pulls a black dress from the rack for Ellen.

But as Nana pulls the dress from the rack,
Tom the cat is spooked.

He jumps from a stack of boxes and bumps
into the attic lamp.

The lamp tips and lands at the top of the attic steps.

The light clicks off. The attic is black.

A SPOOK

Just then, big steps "CLOMP, CLOMP, CLOMP," up into the attic.

Ellen and Jon gasp and hug Nana tight. "What is it Nana?" they ask.

The steps stop. The light clicks back on...

It is just Gramps!

He has a bucket filled with Halloween treats.

TRICK-OR-TREATS

Nana and Gramps stand on the front steps
and hand out treats.

The kids yell, "Trick-or-treat!" as Gramps drops treats
into their bags.

The kids tell Nana and Gramps,
"Thank you," and, "Happy Halloween!"
as they go off into the Halloween night.

Hand-in-hand, Ellen and Jon and Mom and Dad
set out to trick-or-treat too.

When they get back, Ellen and Jon sit
on the front steps next to their jack-o-lanterns.

As they snack on their treats they plan
what they will dress up as next Halloween.

It was a fantastic Halloween Night.

It is Halloween! is decodable with the 26 phonetic alphabet sounds and the ability to blend those sounds together.

Puzzle Words are words used in the story that are either irregular or may have sound/spelling correspondences that the reader may not be familiar with.

The **Puzzle Word Review List** contains Puzzle Words that have been introduced in previous books in the *Books to Remember* Series.

Please Note: If all of the Puzzle Words (sight words) on this page are pre-taught and the reader knows the 26 phonetic alphabet sounds and can blend those sounds together, this book is 100% phonetically decodable.

Puzzle Words:	Puzzle Word Review List:	Decodable Vocabulary:		
do	the	jack	clicks	lands
this	they	it	lamp	at
was	with	is	back	top
thank you	her	and	big	clicks
Halloween	them	Jon	black	off
spook	she	Ellen	trunk	just
jack-o-lantern	then	Gramps	brass	clomp
trick-or-treat	when	pick	lock	gasp
night	into	pumpkins	as	hug
light	too	until	unlocks	stop
tight	what	fill	lifts	Nana's
	he	red	lid	bucket
	their	wagon	hats	stand
	go	helps	masks	hand
	happy	cut	dress-up	kids
	for	biggest	picks	yell
	to	will	ten-gallon	trick
	out	sit	bandana	drops
	of	on	mask	bags
	a	steps	red	tell
	pulls	attic	bonnet	set
		Nana	hands	snack
		asks	vest	plan
		visit	front	fantastic
		not	dress	Mom
		run	from	Dad
		tells	rack	Get
		skip	but	Next
		up	jumps	Gramps'
		cat	stack	
		Tom	boxes	
		runs	bumps	
		in	tips	

"ed" endings:

fill**ed**
spook**ed**